Contents

Animal Power

Thousands of years ago, the only way people traveled was by walking. Then they learned to ride animals from one place to another. Traveling became much easier when an ancient people, called the Sumerians, invented the wheel. Animals could then pull carts carrying people and loads. Today, animals still help people travel and do their work.

Inventing the wheel

The first wheels were made of solid wood. They were strong but heavy, and turned slowly. Over time, half-solid wheels were made. These were lighter and turned more easily. Wheels with **spokes**, the lightest wheels of all, are as strong as solid ones.

Taming animals

Most animals must be tamed and trained before being taught to carry loads or people. An animal that pulls a cart learns to wear a harness that attaches to the cart.

▼ Llamas have cloven, or split, hooves, which help them grip as they travel along mountain paths.

▲ These horses are pulling a stagecoach full of passengers and their baggage.

TRAVELING
on Land

DEBORAH CHANCELLOR

TWO CAN ™

PRINCETON ■ LONDON

How to use this book

Cross-references
Above some of the chapter titles, you will find a list of other chapters in the book that are related to the topic. Turn to these pages to find out more about each subject.

See for yourself
See-for-yourself bubbles give you the chance to test out some of the ideas in this book. They explain what you will need and what you have to do to see if an idea really works.

Quiz corner
In the quiz corner, you will find a list of questions. The answers to the quiz questions are somewhere in the same chapter. Try to answer all the questions about each topic.

Chatterboxes
Chatterboxes give you interesting facts about other things that are related to the subject.

Glossary
Difficult words are explained in the glossary on page 31. These words are in **bold** type in the book. Look them up in the glossary to find out what they mean.

Index
The index is on page 32. It is a list of important words mentioned in the book, with page numbers next to the entries. If you want to read about a subject, look it up in the index, then turn to the page number given.

Working animals

In many parts of the world, animals are used to do work that people find difficult. Some animals, such as elephants, can move loads that are too heavy for people to carry. Other animals, such as llamas and camels, are useful because they can travel to places that cars and trucks cannot reach.

▲ Elephants in Thailand have been trained to move heavy logs with their trunks.

look at: Motorcycles, page 8

Bicycles

A bicycle is a simple machine that has two wheels. You make it move by turning the pedals with your feet. A bicycle is cheap to run and does not **pollute** the air. This is because it has no **engine**. All around the world, adults and children ride bicycles, especially in places where cars cannot go.

Changing to a low **gear** *makes it easier for the rider to pedal uphill.*

The handlebars let the rider steer and balance the bike.

The brakes rub against the wheel to slow down the bike.

▲ This cyclist is stunt riding. He is wearing padded clothing, a helmet and safety goggles to protect him if he falls off.

An American named Steve Roberts has invented the world's strangest bicycle. It has four computers and a refrigerator on board, which are all powered by the sun's rays.

*The chain carries **power** to the back wheel and makes the wheel turn.*

*Tires grip the road better because they have a rough pattern on them called **tread**.*

The pedals are linked to the back wheel by the chain.

Bikes for hire

In some countries, people use pedicabs to travel around town. These are similar to bicycles but usually have three wheels. People pay the pedicab operator to take them to where they want to go.

▲ Often, it is quicker and cheaper to travel by pedicab than by car or taxi.

Quiz Corner

● Do bicycles pollute the air?

● What does a bicycle chain do?

● Which part of a bicycle lets you steer and helps you balance?

● What is the pattern on a tire called?

look at: Bicycles, page 6

Motorcycles

A motorcycle is similar to a bicycle, but it is powered by a gasoline **engine**. It is also stronger than a bicycle and can travel faster. In 1885, the first motorcycle was built in Germany by Gottlieb Daimler. It could travel at about eight miles per hour. Today, motorcycles can reach much higher speeds. The world record is 322.87 miles per hour.

CHATTERBOX

How many people do you think can balance on one motorcycle? In 1987 in New South Wales, Australia, 47 people managed to ride on a single bike.

A biker must wear a helmet to protect his head in case of an accident. ....

A shield made of tough, clear plastic protects the biker from the wind. ....

A biker wears strong leather clothing to protect his body and keep him warm. ....

Gripping the ground

As a motorcycle moves along, rough **tread** on the tire causes **friction** between the tire and the ground. Friction helps the tire to grip the ground.

▼ The tires on trail bikes have an especially deep tread to help them grip rough, wet and muddy ground.

Tread on the tires gives more grip on wet roads.

Trail bikes

Not all motorcycles are built to be ridden on roads. A trail bike can travel across rough country, even in places where there are no dirt tracks. It can also climb hills and cross streams.

Quiz Corner

● Who built the first motorcycle?

● Why do motorcycle tires have tread?

● What kind of a motorcycle can climb hills and cross streams?

look at: Roads, page 20; In the Future, page 28

Cars

One of the easiest and quickest ways to travel is by car. Like motorcycles, most cars have gasoline **engines**. Inside the engine, gasoline burns to make **energy**, which turns the wheels. The first car with a gasoline engine was built in 1885 by a German named Karl Benz. It had three wheels and moved very slowly.

Streamlined cars
Engineers try to design cars with a **streamlined**, or smooth and rounded, shape. Streamlined cars let air flow over them easily, helping them to travel quickly. Cars which are not streamlined use more **fuel** to travel at the same rate of speed.

In most cars, the engine is at the front of the car, under the hood.

At night, drivers use headlights to see the road ahead. Turn signals at the side of the car show when it is about to turn left or right.

Drivers use the steering wheel to turn the car.

Seat belts help protect drivers and passengers if they are in an accident.

Designed for speed

A race car has a very streamlined shape to help it travel at high speeds. The driver sits strapped into a snug seat.

◀ During a race, mechanics work quickly to change the car's tires and fill it up with fuel.

Busy roads

Today, there are more cars on the road than ever before. In cities around the world, such as Mexico City, Mexico, there are sometimes so many cars on the road, that nobody can move. This is called gridlock.

At night, tail lights make the car visible from behind.

Quiz Corner

● Who built the first car with a gasoline engine?

● Why must race cars have a streamlined shape?

● What is it called when there are so many cars on the road that nobody can move?

look at: Cars, page 10; Trains, page 22; In the Future, page 28

Buses and Trolleys

If more people traveled by bus instead of by car, there would be less traffic on the roads. Buses carry lots of people at one time. They are good for short trips around town and for traveling long distances. One bus uses less **fuel** than if all the people on board traveled in their own cars.

Public transportation

Most cities have a group of buses that people pay to use. This is one type of public transportation. Each bus follows a different **route**, usually marked by a different number. People wait for the bus along the route at bus stops. When people get on the bus, they pay for their trip.

▼ This bus is on a route through London, England. It has two **decks** and can carry about ninety people.

15 Canning Town Poplar
Aldgate St Pauls
Aldwych Trafalgar Sq

CANNING TOWN

EAST LONDON

TOWER BRIDGE

RML 2456

JJD 456D

Long-distance travel

Some large buses, called coaches, travel long distances, from one city to another. They are designed to make journeys as pleasant as possible. They have toilets and soft seats, and sometimes they even show videos on board.

Trolleys

In some cities there are trolleys as well as buses. Trolleys run along steel rails that are sunk into the road. They are a good type of public transportation because they cause very little **pollution**.

Quiz Corner

- Name a type of public transportation.
- How do some trolleys pick up electricity?
- Where could you catch a ride on the world's longest bus route?
- Why are trolleys a good type of public transportation?

◀ Around the world, many buses are decorated and brightly painted. They can be very crowded.

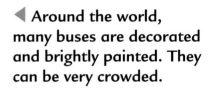

How trolleys work

Trolleys are powered by electricity. Some trolleys are run by a frame on the roof, called a pantograph, which picks up electricity from cables running high above the street.

pantograph

cables

CHATTERBOX

Caracas

The world's longest bus route is in South America, between Buenos Aires, Argentina and Caracas, Venezuela. It is 6,003 miles long and takes about nine days, including stops.

Buenos Aires

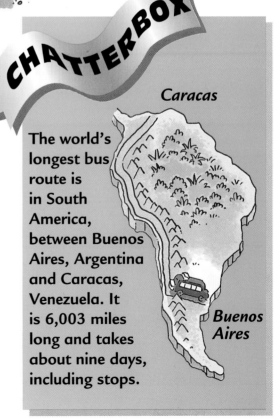

13

Keeping things moving

New traffic control systems are being designed to help keep **vehicles** moving on busy roads. Cameras and computers can let traffic police know about problems such as traffic jams and accidents so that they can quickly go to help.

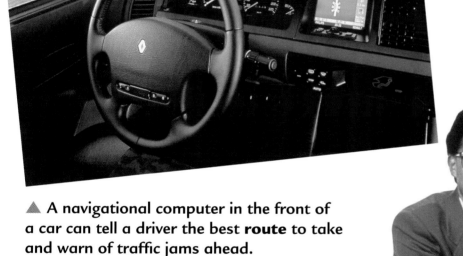

▲ A navigational computer in the front of a car can tell a driver the best **route** to take and warn of traffic jams ahead.

What next?

All the time, scientists are busy designing different vehicles to carry people and goods. These new types of transportation might look strange now, but soon you might see them in towns and cities everywhere.

▶ This tiny car fits inside a special suitcase. When it is not being driven, it can be folded away and carried.

Quiz Corner

● From where do solar-powered cars take their energy?

● Why is it important to use public transportation?

● Why are navigational computers useful for drivers?

Amazing Facts

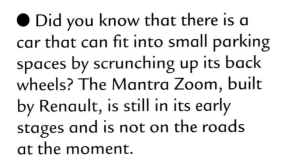

● Did you know that there is a car that can fit into small parking spaces by scrunching up its back wheels? The Mantra Zoom, built by Renault, is still in its early stages and is not on the roads at the moment.

☆ *The power of an engine is measured in units called horsepower. This is because the power of an engine is compared to the pulling power of a horse — so a one-horsepower engine is as powerful as one horse.*

● Huskies really need their thick coats to keep them warm. At night, these dogs do not sleep in kennels but dig themselves beds in the snow.

☆ *In Italy, there is a train that has been specially designed to lean inward when it goes around corners. This means that the train does not have to slow down as much for curves, making journeys faster.*

● The largest train station in the world is Grand Central Station in New York City. It is built on two levels with forty-one tracks on the upper level and twenty-six on the lower level.

☆ *An American named Henry Ford was the first car manufacturer to build cars on an assembly line. Here, ready-made parts for each car are fitted together at different places along a moving line. Each mechanic has to do just one job, so the cars can be built very quickly.*

● The world's longest car is a twenty-six wheeled limousine, built in California. It is one hundred feet long and has an enormous water bed and a swimming pool in the back.

☆ *Mexico City has some of the world's worst traffic jams. It also has over 60,000 taxis, which is more than any other city in the world.*

Glossary

deck Each floor of a **vehicle**, such as a bus.

diesel A type of fuel used in some **engines**.

energy What gives living things or machines the **power** to do a job, such as to make an **engine** go.

engine A machine that changes **energy** into motion.

engineer Someone who designs things that are useful to people.

environment The world around us.

freight Goods moved from place to place by train, truck or ship.

friction The force caused by two surfaces rubbing together. When tires rub against a road surface, friction slows the wheels.

fuel Any substance that is burned to make heat or **energy**. **Engines** need fuel to make them work.

gear A device that changes the speed at which the wheels of a **vehicle** turn when the same amount of **energy** is being used.

pollute To spoil air, soil or water with garbage or other harmful things.

pollution Waste and unhealthy things dumped into the **environment**.

power The strength to do a job.

route The way you take to travel to a particular place.

siren A machine which makes a warning sound on an emergency **vehicle.**

spokes Thin bars that join the center, or hub, of a wheel to its outside, or rim.

streamlined Having a shape that lets air or water flow easily over it. A race car is streamlined to reduce air **friction**, making it as fast as possible.

tread The bumpy pattern on a tire, that helps the wheel to get a good grip on the road. The tread also pushes water away, making tires less likely to slip on wet roads.

vehicle Something used to carry people or goods from one place to another.

Index

www.two-canpublishing.com

Published in the United States
and Canada by
Two-Can Publishing LLC
234 Nassau Street
Princeton, NJ 08542
in arrangement with
C.D. Stampley Enterprises, Inc.

© 2001, 1997 Two-Can Publishing
For information on Two-Can books
and multimedia, call 1-609-921-6700,
fax 1-609-921-3349, or visit our Web site
at http://www.two-canpublishing.com

Text: Deborah Chancellor
Consultant: Eryl Davies
Watercolor artwork: Colin King
and Stuart Trotter
Computer artwork: D Oliver
Commissioned photography:
Steve Gorton
Photo Research: Dipika
Palmer-Jenkins
Editorial Director: Jane Wilsher
Art Director: Carole Orbell
Production Director: Lorraine Estelle
Project Manager: Eljay Yildirim
Editor: Deborah Kespert
Assistant Editors: Julia Hillyard,
Claire Yude
Co-edition Editor: Leila Peerun

'Two-Can' is a trademark of Two-Can
Publishing. Two-Can Publishing is a
division of Zenith Entertainment Ltd,
43-45 Dorset Street, London W1H 4AB

hc ISBN 1-58728-2208
sc ISBN 1-58728-2143

hc 1 2 3 4 5 6 7 8 9 10 02 01
sc 1 2 3 4 5 6 7 8 9 10 02 01

Photographic credits: Britstock-IFA
p15tr, p27tl; Colorific p26bl;
Hutchison Library (H.R. Dorig) p4tr;
Image Bank p14bl, p17tl, p19tr;
A.C. Press p29br; Quadrant p14bc;
Spectrum p5; Tony Stone Images
front cover, p8b, p22-23c, p25tr;
Frank Spooner p28b&t, p29tl;
Telegraph Colour Library p18bl;
Zefa p6bl, p7cr, p9, p11t, p12, p26-
27bc.

Printed in USA

Title previously published under
the Launch Pad Library series